Wake Up
ENGINES

by Denise Dowling Mortensen

illustrated by Melissa Iwai

Clarion Books ✳ *New York*

To my mom and dad —D.D.M   For my Jamie, who always wakes up ready to go! Go! GO!—M. I.

Clarion Books • a Houghton Mifflin Company imprint • 215 Park Avenue South, New York, NY 10003 • Text copyright © 2007 by Denise Dowling Mortensen • Illustrations copyright © 2007 by Melissa Iwai • The illustrations were executed in acrylic paint. • The text was set in 26-point Cochin. • All rights reserved. For information about permission to reproduce selections from this book, write to Permissions, Houghton Mifflin Company, 215 Park Avenue South, New York, NY 10003 . • www.clarionbooks.com • Manufactured in China • Library of Congress Cataloging-in-Publication Data • Mortensen, Denise Dowling. • Wake up engines/ by Denise Dowling Mortensen ; illustrated by Melissa Iwai. • p. cm. • Summary: Rhyming verses describe the sights and sounds of morning traffic as cars, trucks, and airplanes rev up their engines and go! • ISBN-13: 978-0-618-51736-7 • ISBN-10: 0-618-51736-7 • [1. Vehicles—Fiction. 2. Transportation—Fiction. 3. Morning Fiction. 4. Stories in rhyme.] I. Iwai, Melissa, ill. II. Title. • PZ8.3.M842Wak 2007 • [E]—dc22 • 2006020921 • WKT 10 9 8 7 6 5 4 3 2

Wake up engines,
brand-new day.

Fasten seatbelt,
drive away.

7

Morning traffic,
motors hum.

HONK! HONK!
TOOT! TOOT!
BRMM! BRMM! BRMM!

8

City sweeper
rumble, hiss.
Scrubbing brushes

SWISH!

SWISH!

SWISH!

Gutters glisten
shiny, clean.
Whirring, purring
street machine.

Yellow school bus,
creaky brakes.
Chilly engine
rattles, shakes.

14

Red lights flashing,
closing door.
Stick shift
ready?
RUMBLE!
     ROOOAR!

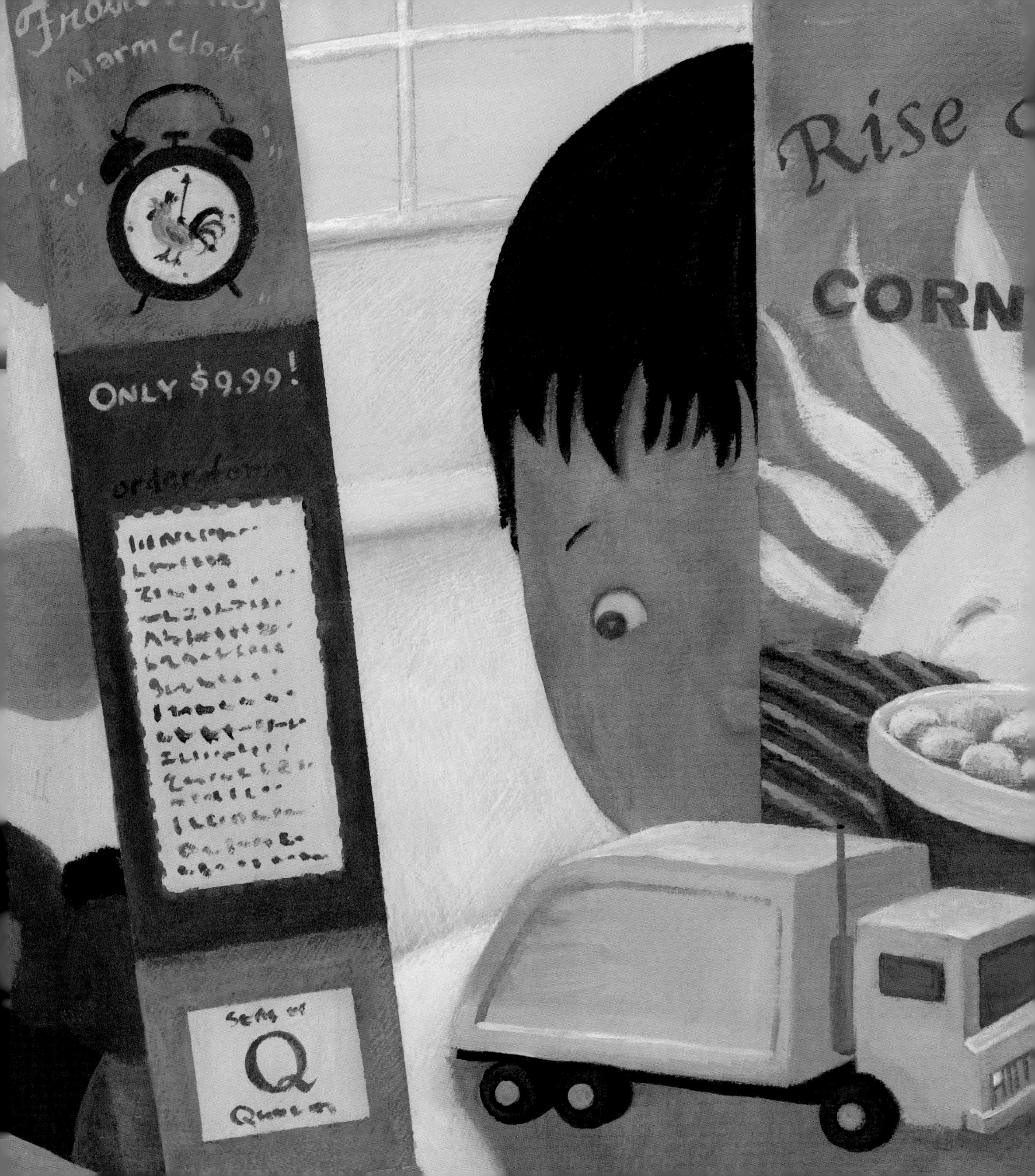
Alarm Clock
ONLY $9.99!
Rise
CORN
Q

Garbage truck
with empty loader.
Alley-crawling
diesel motor.

19

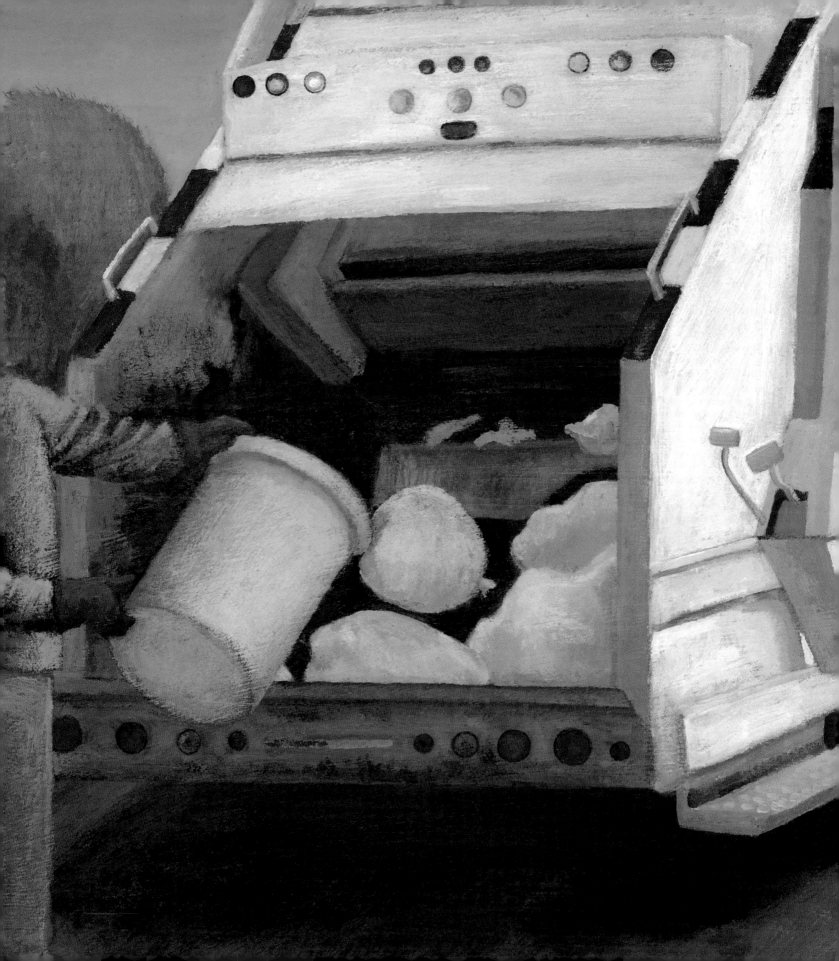

Trash-can thunder,
sooty plume.
Grinding lever.
BOOM! BOOM! BOOM!

Traffic chopper,
rooftop nest.
Rotors spinning,
preflight test.

23

Volume heavy,
morning glare.
Cleared for takeoff.
THUMP! THUMP!

Air.

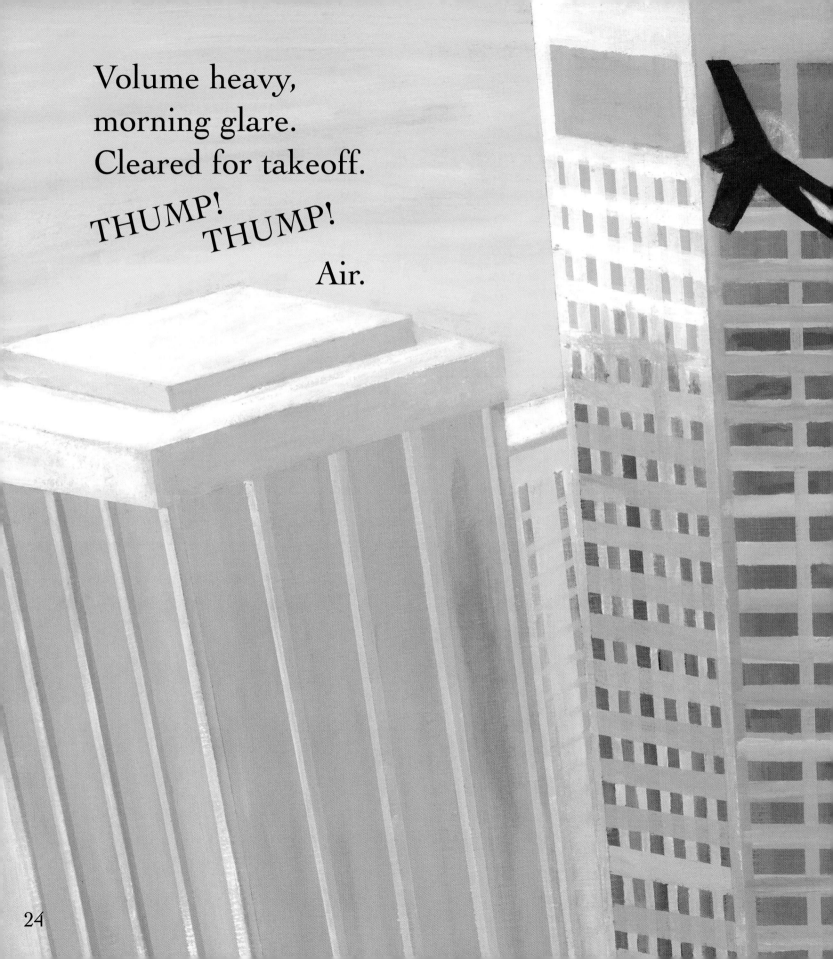

26

Flight 180
next in line.
Forward throttle,
turbo whine.

Down the runway,
zooming fast.
Nose up,
lift off.
VROOM! VROOM!
BLAAAAST!

29

Busy engines
wide awake.
Roads to travel,
flights to take.

Morning traffic,
fast or slow.
Wake up engines,
GO! GO! GO!